THIS ANNUAL BELONGS TO...

Published 2021.
Little Brother Books Ltd, Ground Floor,
23 Southernhay East, Exeter, Devon EX1 1QL
books@littlebrotherbooks.co.uk | www.littlebrotherbooks.co.uk

Printed in Poland. ul. Połczyńska 99,01303 Warszawa.

LittleBrother BOOKS

FSC
MIX
Paper from responsible sources
FSC® C016890

WELCOME TO...
CRETACIA!

In a prehistoric land long ago, four dinosaur friends have all sorts of fun and adventures. When they're not playing, creating or exploring, Rocky, Bill, Tiny and Mazu are keeping their eyes and ears open for Gigantosaurus!

ROARRR!

This big bad monster often pops up when they least expect it and he's always hungry. Not much is known about the mysterious Giganto, but smart dinos know to keep out of his way.

CONTENTS

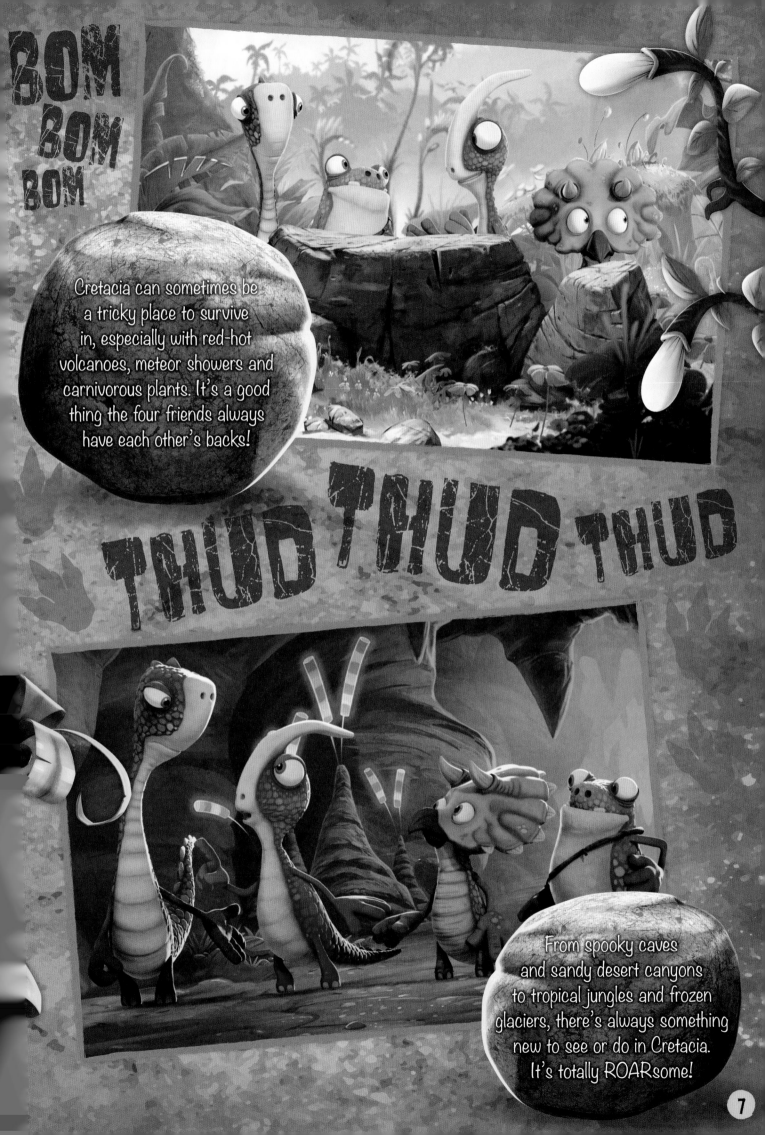

BOM BOM BOM

Cretacia can sometimes be a tricky place to survive in, especially with red-hot volcanoes, meteor showers and carnivorous plants. It's a good thing the four friends always have each other's backs!

THUD THUD THUD

From spooky caves and sandy desert canyons to tropical jungles and frozen glaciers, there's always something new to see or do in Cretacia. It's totally ROARsome!

GIGANTO

ALL ABOUT... GIGANTOSAURUS

Mysterious and scary, Gigantosaurus is the most dangerous predator of the Cretaceous period. He spends his time stomping around searching for food or snoring loudly. One thing's for sure... you never know when he will suddenly pop up!

When he's on the hunt for food, every other creature gets out of Giganto's way. No one wants to end up as tasty lunch snack for that monster mouth.

What's that loud rumbling? It's just Gigantosaurus having a sleep. He can doze through almost anything and his snores are as loud as a volcano!

Giganto's only real problem is when he needs to scratch his back. With his tiny arms, the only solution is to use a handy tree for a quick rub!

HOW GIGANTO GOT HIS ROAR

Rocky wants to roar as loudly as Gigantosaurus, so he and Marshall set out to capture the beast's roar inside a coconut. Now they just need Giganto to help them out...

In the cave one day, the little dinos were having a roaring contest. Mazu went first. Her roar echoed loudly around the cave. Bill had a try next, and managed to scare himself! But when Rocky took his turn, only the softest of roars would come out! Rocky's cheeks turned red.

"Don't worry, Rocky," said Mazu. "Your roar will get louder as you get older." But Rocky wanted to roar loudly now, just like Giganto!

"We'll have to catch Giganto's roar then," said Marsh.

"Just like in the bedtime story tha Grandpa Stego tells me." Marsh told story about how when Giganto was little dino, he couldn't roar. So Gigan went into a cave where a huge, scar dino lived, and captured its roar in a coconut shell. Then he opened the coconut, and swallowed the mighty r

"Hmm," said Mazu, but Rocky believed every word of the story.

"Let's go find Giganto!" said Roc

So off went Rocky and Marsh, in search of Gigantosaurus and his mighty roar. They didn't have to go far before they tracked down the big dino, but Giganto was fast asleep.

"He's snoring, not roaring! We'll have to wait," said Rocky, disappointed. But when Giganto woke up and roared a huge roar, Rocky dropped his coconut shells in fright. Giganto stomped away through the jungle with the two little dinosaurs trying their best to keep up.

The next time Rocky tried to capture Giganto's roar was even worse – Rocky was blasted through the air and landed by Termy's lake.

"Whenever I want something, I sing the Please and Thank You song," Marshall told his friend. So when Giganto came along for a cool drink, Rocky began to sing:

"Hey Giganto, what you waitin' for? 'Please' and 'thank you' – now give me a ROAR!" But this time, instead of roaring at Rocky, Giganto stomped softly away.

A little later, Mazu, Tiny and Bill arrived at the lake. They had collected some mossy snacks for Giganto, but the big dino was nowhere to be seen.

"Termy, have you seen Giganto?" asked Mazu.

"Yes," Termy replied. "Rocky and that stego are chasing him, to capture Giganto's roar." The little dinos were shocked!

"Don't they know that's just a bedtime story?" said Mazu.

"We have to find them!" added Tiny.

Meanwhile, Rocky and Marsh had reached the canyon.

"Giganto! WAIT!" called Rocky. Rocky's voice echoed back through the rocky canyon. Then he had an idea – they could use the echo to get Giganto's attention! So Rocky and Marsh roared their loudest roars. "ROOAARRR!" Giganto growled back. Rocky clapped his coconut shells together to capture Giganto's roar, but all he caught was a dragonfly! Then there was trouble... a scary scorpion was heading Marsh's way!

"Help!" cried Marsh. "Do something, Rocky!" Even without Giganto's roar, Rocky knew he had to save his friend. So he let out the longest, loudest roar he had ever roared – it was as scary as Giganto's and echoed out across all of Cretacia! Shocked, the scorpion turned and scuttled away.
   "You did it, Rocky!" cheered Marsh. "You saved me!"

Mazu, Tiny and Bill arrived moments later.
   "Where's Giganto? We just heard his roar," said Mazu.
   "That was me," smiled Rocky proudly. "Turns out I didn't need to catch Giganto's roar, after all. It was inside me the whole time!" Marsh turned to his friend.
   "Rocky, could you do that big roar again?" he asked. Rocky was puzzled – Marsh wasn't in danger any more.
   "I want to capture YOUR roar for myself!" Marsh smiled. And Rocky's friends all smiled too!

DRIVER DASH

BILL

Use a stop watch and see how long it takes you to guide my friends to their vehicles. Write your times in the boxes! Who was the fastest?

A

B

C

1

2

3

WORD SEARCH CHALLENGE

Can you find the eight words hidden in the grid below? Don't forget to look forwards, backwards, up, down and diagonally!

GIGANTO **BILL** **MAZU** **CROR**
ROCKY **TINY** **TREY** **TOTOR**

```
A R O T O T O T C R A M V
N Y D T P O Y E R T P B I
T S I G N T C U O R H I F
J N A P T A H G R K M L U
Y H Y S D N G Z J A O L B
O V I Z B U C I T E S K P
T G U Z A M U O G U C R O
J S V E U T O T R O Y P D
D F H S R O C K Y E L Y I
G I G A S N O T S F B Y C
```

Now find the special coloured letters and unscramble them to reveal a secret character!

Answers on page 76.

Can you spot 10 differences between these two pictures? Colour in a dino footprint for each one you find!

MAZU

WHO'S THAT DINO?

TINY

Something strange has happened to this picture! Can you work out who is in it? Write your answer below.

Answer on page 76.

MARVELLOUS MAZE

It looks like Bill is lost! Help guide him through this tricky maze and reach his friends by the lake.

Answer on page 76.

FINISH

START

ALL ABOUT... ROCKY

ROCKY

Type: Parasaurolophus
Age: 9 years old
Strengths: Good legs for running
Weaknesses: Often ends up in Giganto's den!
Dreams of: Fighting Gigantosaurus and becoming a superhero

Brave and bursting with lots of energy, Rocky wants to be a superhero and tackle the biggest villain he can find... Gigantosaurus!

Rocky often jumps in before thinking, which can land him in all sorts of trouble. It's a good thing his dino friends are always there to help him out!

Thanks to his good legs, Rocky can run really fast. They often come in handy when he's being chased by Gigantosaurus!

Rocky leads the gang into lots of new adventures. Loyal and brave, this plucky parasaurolophus always takes care of Bill, Tiny and Mazu!

GIGANTO POWER

When Mazu makes Rocky a Giganto tail, Rocky quickly learns that having a giant tail is a big responsibility!

One morning, the little dinos were playing a game to see who could hit a coconut the furthest using their tail. Bill threw the first coconut to Tiny, whose strong tail whacked it for Hegan to catch. Next up was Mazu. Her shot flew through the air, travelling even further than Tiny's. But when Rocky took his turn, the coconut span out of control, causing Hegan to crash-land on top of Bill!

"I wish I could hit the ball like you, Mazu," Rocky sighed. But there was one tail that was even stronger than Mazu's, and that belonged to ... **Giganto!** His tail could hit a coconut all the way to the Frozen Land! Mazu wanted to help her friend, and set to work building Rocky a new tail that would be just as powerful as Giganto's.

Before long, the new tail was ready. Tiny and Bill gasped when they saw it.

"Wow! That's huge, are you sure you can control it?" said Bill. As Rocky swished the giant tail this way and that, his friends had to quickly dive out of the way!

"Sorry!" said Rocky. "Once I get the hang of it, I'll use my **giganto-tail** to help dinos all over Cretacia!" he smiled.

Moments later, Rocky's first customer stomped by. Poor Marshall had a prickly bush stuck to his tail.

"Help a dino out?" he moaned.

"**Rocky to the rescue!**" smiled Rocky.

With a flick of his giganto-tail, he sent Marshall and the bush flying. They landed with a **bump**, but the prickly bush was still stuck fast. "Aww, coconuts!" Rocky cried.

Later that day, Rocky was on a mission to help more dinos. Soon, he spotted Cror and Totor, trying to steal Rugo's pickled peppers. But when Rocky tried to help, his tail began to slam up and down wildly. The ground shook, bouncing the pickles straight into the claws of the greedy raptors.

"My pickled picnic peppers!" cried Rugo.

"I'm sorry," said Rocky sadly.

Rocky felt terrible. "I thought having this tail would give me super powers, but instead it's causing super problems," he told his friends.

"You were just trying to help," Tiny said kindly.

"That's right," Bill agreed. "Maybe only Giganto can handle that kind of power?"

He knew his dino friends were probably right, but Rocky wasn't about to give up just yet!

Next, Rocky tried to help Iggy move his boulder to a sunny spot. But the powerful tail smashed the boulder into a pillar that was holding up a rocky ledge! Rocky summoned all his strength to hold up the pillar with his tail, before Giganto fetched a tree to make the ledge safe. Tiny, Bill and Mazu were impressed.

"You really are a superhero, Rocky!" they smiled.

"Thanks," smiled Rocky. "But I think it's time to give up the Giganto tail. Having all that power is hard work. I'll stick with my own tail from now on."

Before they put the tail away, though, there was time for one last game. This time, Rocky smashed his coconut all the way to Frozen Land for a **Giganto home run!**

As his friends cheered, Rocky beamed with pride.

DINO DRAWING

Copy the picture of Rocky below into the blank frame. Try drawing one square at a time to make it easier.

BILL

Now colour in your finished picture!

MAZU MASK

Impress your friends by making and wearing this awesome Mazu mask!

1. Ask an adult to help you make your mask. Cut along the dotted lines.
2. Carefully cut around the mask. Cut out the eye and side holes.
3. Don't want to cut up your book? Photocopy or scan and print the page instead.
4. Measure and cut a length of string to fit around the back of your head. Feed the ends of the string through the side holes and secure with knots.

Ask an adult for help making your Mazu mask!

Try decorating this side of the mask with pens, pencils and crayons!

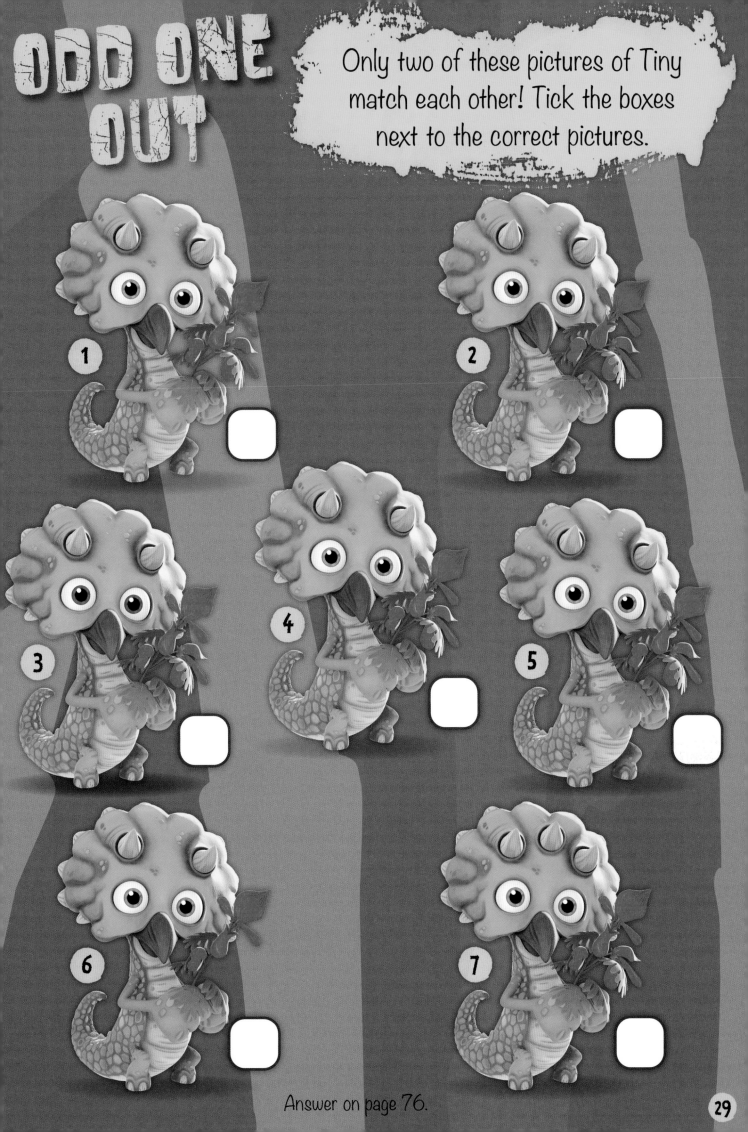

ODD ONE OUT

Only two of these pictures of Tiny match each other! Tick the boxes next to the correct pictures.

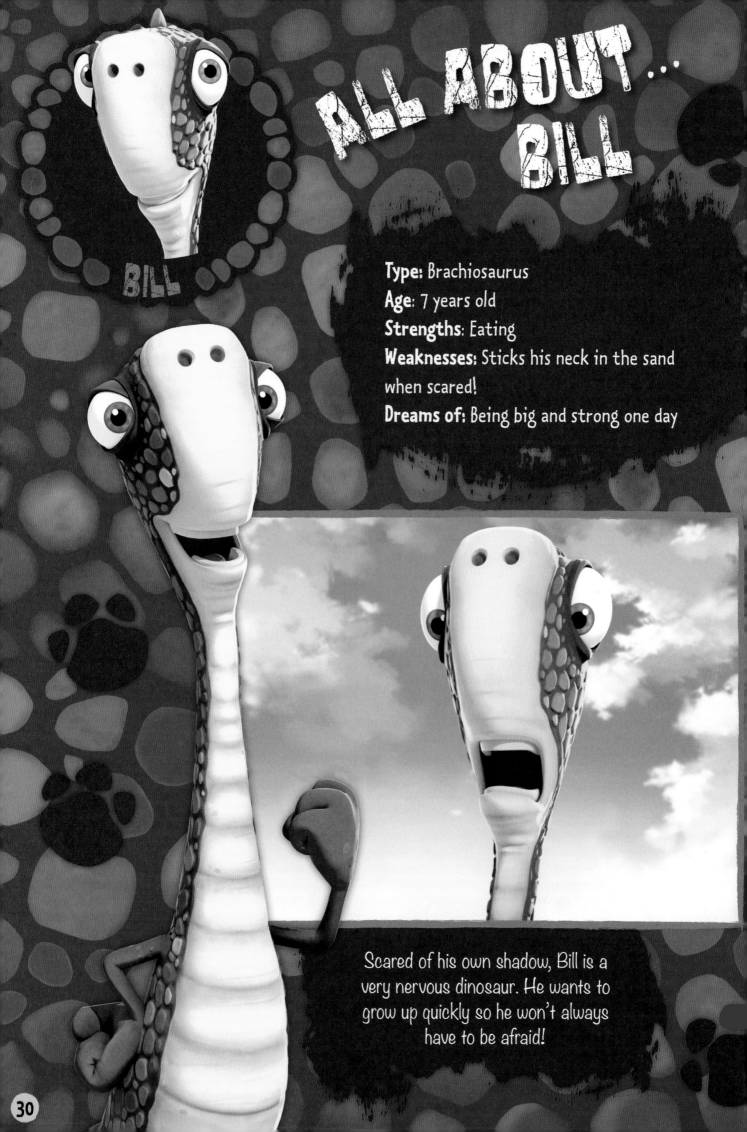

ALL ABOUT... BILL

BILL

Type: Brachiosaurus
Age: 7 years old
Strengths: Eating
Weaknesses: Sticks his neck in the sand when scared!
Dreams of: Being big and strong one day

Scared of his own shadow, Bill is a very nervous dinosaur. He wants to grow up quickly so he won't always have to be afraid!

Bill doesn't like taking risks, but his friends keep getting him into scary situations. Good thing Bill has a long neck... perfect for being on the lookout!

The only way Bill is going to grow up to be a fully grown brachiosaurus is by eating. No wonder he's always so hungry!

The biggest danger in Bill's timid life is Gigantosaurus. Why does that huge dinosaur have to have such sharp teeth and scary claws?

A TINY TRIUMPH

When the dino friends get lost in the desert, will Tiny's artistic talents be enough to save the day?

It was another fine day in Cretacia. In the shadow of Mount Oblivion, Gigantosaurus was enjoying splashing in the water of a hot spring. The little dinos were having fun too, playing a game. Whoever could sneak the closest to Giganto would be the winner! Rocky and Mazu bravely ran towards Giganto's tail – and both touched it at once! Bill was right behind them, but Tiny was nowhere to be seen.

Just then, Tiny appeared from behind a boulder. She had been busily drawing an amazing dinosaur picture on the rock.

"Hey! How about we play Art Show next?" she suggested. Her friends were puzzled.

"Is that even a game?" wondered Rocky. But before Tiny could reply, there came the most enormous rumble. The volcano was erupting and red-hot lava was heading their way! "RUN!" yelled Mazu.

Seconds later, Hegan swooped overhead. "Looks like you could use a lift!" the flying dino chirped. Rocky, Mazu, Bill and Tiny gratefully scrambled onto Hegan's back.

"Phew! That was close!" said Bill. Giganto had run far away from the lava, too. Everyone was safe! Suddenly, a leaf blew through the breeze, and landed on Rocky's face. Tiny had an idea . . . on the leaf, she began to sketch out everything she could see below.

"What a beautiful view," said Tiny. "Who knew there was a river in the desert?"

Hegan found a safe place to land, far away from the volcano. The dinos began to explore . . . there were all sorts of interesting flowers and rocks to look at.

"I'm so thirsty!" said Bill. "Let's find that river we saw," said Rocky. But no one was sure which way to go.

"Maybe we could play Art Show?" said Tiny, holding up her leaf.

"Tiny!" smiled Mazu. "You've drawn a map – and there's the river, look!"

With Mazu reading the map, the dinos set off to find the river. Tiny had collected some colourful flowers that she didn't want to leave behind, so she dragged them along behind her.

"The map says to go this way, through the canyon," said Mazu. But guarding the entrance to the rocky canyon were some fierce-looking plants!

"We can't go through there, those are dino-eating plants!" warned Bill.

"Too bad we're not plants," said Mazu. "Then they wouldn't eat us."

Tiny had another bright idea. "Then let's be plants, too!" she smiled, sharing out the leaves and petals she had collected earlier. Soon, everyone was wearing a flowery disguise.

"I really hope this is going to work!" said Bill. He felt very silly dressed up as a daisy!

Together, the four dinos crept past the huge plants. The plan had worked!

The dinos walked on through the desert, until at last they found the river, and a cool drink! In the water, Tiny spotted a sparkly gemstone! Bill and Rocky found more gems, too. The dinos were just admiring their treasure, when along stomped Giganto.

"Where's Hegan to get us out of here?" cried Bill. Clever Tiny knew what to do – she quickly arranged the gems to make a picture of dinosaur. Then while Giganto stopped to look at the glistening jewels, Hegan flapped down to rescue her friends.

"We'd never have made it without all your clever pictures and costumes, Tiny," smiled Mazu. "Your art is amazing!" Rocky agreed. So when the dinos arrived home safe and sound, everyone wanted to play Tiny's game at last – Art Show! Dinos came from far and wide to check out Tiny's creations, including a giant unexpected guest. What did Giganto think of his portrait? ROARsome, of course!

DINO DOT TO DOT

Join the dots to reveal the mystery dino!
Now use your favourite pens, pencils and
crayons to decorate your picture.

MAZU

36

LETTER TRACING

Trace over the letters in the names of these dino friends using your finger or a pencil. Start at the white dots on each letter.

Rocky

Bill

Mazu

Tiny

Now use a pen to follow each letter!

COLOUR GIGANTO

Grab your pens, pencils and paints and colour in this ROARsome picture of my pal, Giganto!

ROCKY

SNEAKY SHADOWS

Draw a line to connect each character to their shadow. Which shadow is the odd one out?

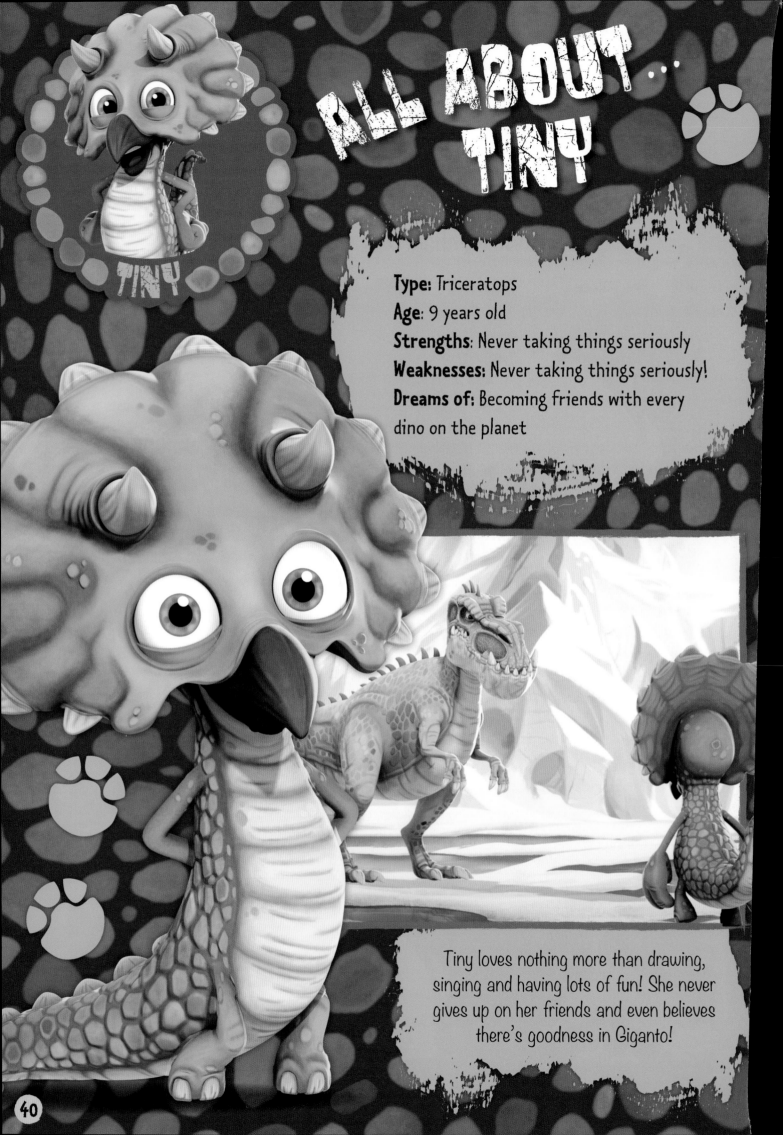

ALL ABOUT... TINY

Type: Triceratops
Age: 9 years old
Strengths: Never taking things seriously
Weaknesses: Never taking things seriously!
Dreams of: Becoming friends with every dino on the planet

Tiny loves nothing more than drawing, singing and having lots of fun! She never gives up on her friends and even believes there's goodness in Giganto!

TINY

Tiny actually invented rock painting and you can see her works of art all over Cretacia. She loves nature and anything that's beautiful!

Tiny may be super-positive, but she just can't stand getting all dirty. She much prefers staying clean and brushing her teeth.

Tiny dreams of a better world where dinos all live in peace and try not to eat each other. Just try telling that to Gigantosaurus!

CRYING WOLFASAURUS

When Bill discovers 'crying wolf' to get what he wants, will anyone believe him when Giganto really shows up?

One morning, the dinos were heading to the Lookout for a picnic. Bill was struggling with his picnic basket – he'd brought enough food to feed a dinosaur three times his size! Just then, Gigantosaurus stomped by.

"Help! Giganto!" cried Bill, diving behind a bush. Giganto disappeared, but Bill was feeling too scared to go on. So his friends picked up Bill and his picnic and carried him on their way.

Soon, they arrived at the bottom of the cliff.

"All we have to do is climb this vine, and we're there!" Rocky explained. Bill wasn't sure.

"That's a long way up," he sa[id] "Why don't we just eat here?" Rocky had an idea… if they sen[t] the food up first, then Bill would be interested! But as Rocky began hoisting up the yummy picnic, there came a loud CRASH! nearby. "GIGANTO!" cried Bill again.

But the noise wasn't Giganto this time! It was just Rugo, trying to crack open a walnut. "Oops!" said Bill.

"I see how you could get Rugo and Giganto mixed up!" joked Tiny. Suddenly, Bill's tummy began to rumble – he couldn't wait a second longer and gobbled up every scrap of his picnic. He was just settling down for a nap when Rugo cried,

"Giganto! Giganto!" But there was no sign of the big dinosaur anywhere!

"What's going on, Rugo?" said Bill.

"Well, calling out Giganto got you what you wanted, so I tried it, too!" Rugo replied, before scurrying off with her nut.

"I guess it did..." Bill said to himself. Bill could have all sorts of fun crying Giganto! He tried it again during a game of hide and seek. With the dinos in their hiding spots, Bill smashed a huge boulder on the ground. It landed with a CRASH! "GIGANTO'S COMING!" he called out.

Rocky, Mazu and Tiny rushed out from their hiding places.

"Found you! Found you! Found you!" smiled Bill.

"Hey, not fair," said Rocky. "You said Giganto was here!" Bill shrugged.

"I guess I was wrong," he fibbed. His friends sighed. They decided to head to the geyser for a soak in the warm waters instead.

But when they arrived, the best spots were already taken! "Coconuts!" cried Bill. "We'll be waiting forever." So Bill tried his trick again, smashing down another boulder. "GIGANTO'S COMING!" he shrieked. Seconds later, the geyser was empty and Bill splashed straight in! "You can't keep calling Giganto just to get what you want!" moaned Mazu. Rocky and Tiny agreed.

Just then, Archie flew by. "Hey kids, want to come to our arche-opera tonight?" he smiled. Bill was worried – he didn't like going out in the dark.

"Wait! What's that?" Bill began. "GIGANTO!" Rocky rolled his eyes.

"You can't fool us any more," he said. So that night, Bill went back to his den, while his friends went to the concert. But home alone, who should creep by but Giganto himself! Bill had to warn his friends, and fast!

But this time, no one believed him… until Giganto did appear! Mazu, Rocky and Tiny jumped onto a lily pad, but it floated far away.

"Try calling Giganto now, Bill!" said Tiny. So that's just what Bill did. As the huge dino followed Bill's calls, his friends hitched a lift back to shore! Even though everyone was safe, Bill was sorry.

"If I hadn't cried Giganto all day, you would have believed me when he really did show up!" he said.

"That's OK, Bill," smiled Rocky. "We're just lucky the music brought out Giganto's gentle side!"

SMALL AND TALL!

TINY

Circle the biggest picture in each row.
Draw a cross on the smallest!

Answers on page 76.

CRETACEAN CLOSE UP

Can you guess who is in the close up pictures below? Match the names to the correct pictures!

CROR   RUGO
PATCHY TREY
BILL   MAZU

1

2

3

4

5

6

Answers on page 76.

CRAFTY COUNTING

MAZU

Sneaky Totor and Cror have hidden my inventions in the jungle! Help me find them all by ticking the boxes for each item as you spot them.

Answers on page 77.

PREHISTORIC PATTERNS

Can you draw in the missing item in each pattern sequence below?

A

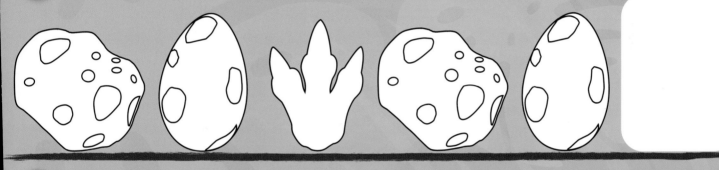

B

C

Answers on page 77.

49

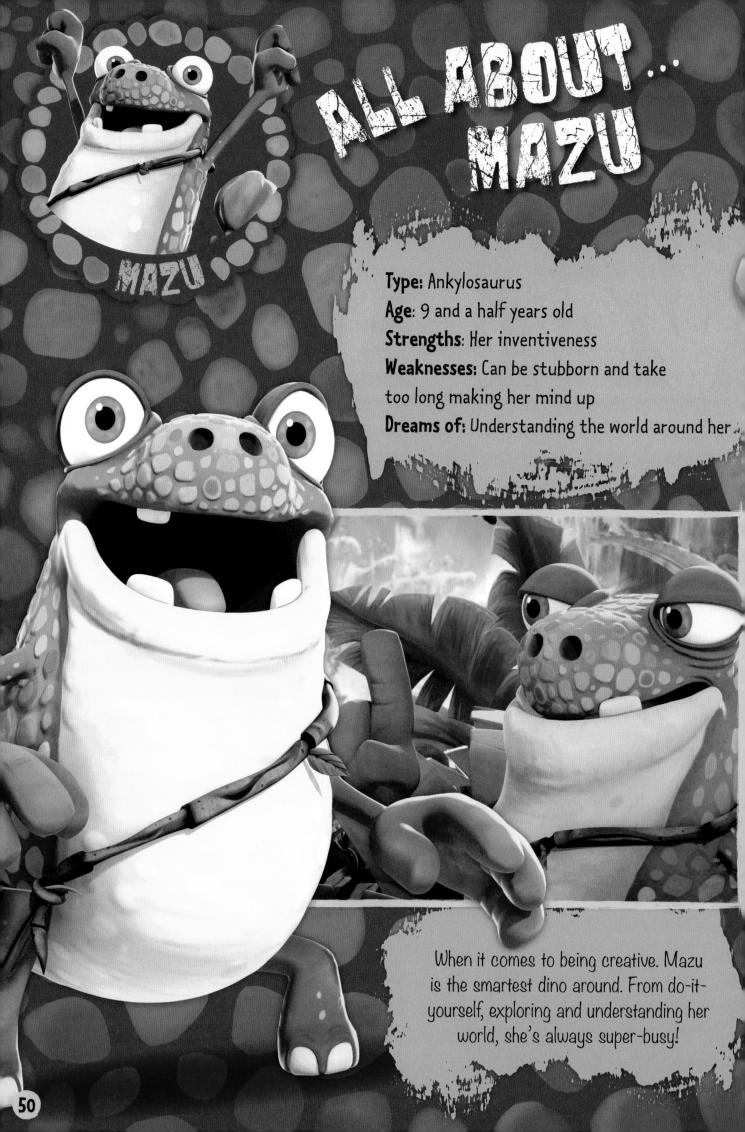

ALL ABOUT... MAZU

MAZU

Type: Ankylosaurus
Age: 9 and a half years old
Strengths: Her inventiveness
Weaknesses: Can be stubborn and take too long making her mind up
Dreams of: Understanding the world around her

When it comes to being creative. Mazu is the smartest dino around. From do-it-yourself, exploring and understanding her world, she's always super-busy!

Mazu loves inventing and creating amazing gadgets. She's sometimes so interested in science though that she doesn't notice what's going on around her!

As an ankylosaurus, Mazu has a boney tail-club, which can sometimes comes in handy as a hammer when she's making stuff!

Mazu is fascinated by Gigantosaurus and would love to catch him so she can study how he hunts and what he eats. Easier said than done!

51

A VERY STICKY PROBLEM

When an accident with some gooey tar leaves Mazu and Cror stuck back-to-back, the two end up bonding like never before!

Mazu was planning a test. She wanted to find out which food Giganto liked best. She had collected some coconuts and a bone, now all Mazu needed was a walnut.
But the perfect nut was high in the tree.

"I'll reach it with my stick-and-picker!" said Mazu. She aimed her arrow and fired. To everyone's surprise, the arrow with fruit dipped in sticky tar stuck to the nut. Then Mazu pulled on her vine rope, and the walnut fell to the ground.

"Wow!" gasped Tiny.

Mazu was just adding the walnut to the pile of food, when Cror and Totor came sniffing by.

"This coconut looks tasty," grinned Cror.

"Give that back!" cried Mazu, chasing after her. Suddenly, Cror slipped down the rocks, tumbling into a pool of tar. A patch of black, sticky goo stuck to Cror's back. Mazu tumbled after her and landed – SPLAT! – on the raptor's back.

"Get off me!" Cror croaked. But Mazu couldn't – she was well and truly stuck!

So Rocky, Tiny and Bill pulled one way while Totor pulled the other, but the tar just stretched and stretched – Mazu and Cror would not come unstuck! "We need a stronger dinosaur to help," cried Cror.

"Like Gigantosaurus?" wondered Mazu.

"Like Gigantosaurus!" smiled Cror, running off into the jungle. Mazu tried to stop Cror, telling her that Giganto was too dangerous, but Cror wouldn't listen. She wanted Mazu off her back as soon as possible!

"Where's Giganto when you need him?" said Cror. Mazu was about to reply when there came a loud rumbling sound. It was Cror's stomach – she was ready for a snack!

"I could reach some fruit for you," Mazu suggested. But Cror had other ideas.

"I've found lunch!" she smiled, licking her lips.

"Bad Cror! That's Patchy's melon!" said Mazu. The naughty raptor snatched the melon in her jaws and ran away.

"Bandit!" Patchy shouted after her.

Before long, Cror was hungry again.

"I can get us some berries if you let me help," said Mazu. At first, Cror didn't believe that someone would be so kind, until Mazu plucked a delicious gooba berry from the tree and tossed it to her.

"Don't you have any friends you trust?" asked Mazu.

"Just my brother," Cror replied between mouthfuls of berry.

Next, Cror feasted on a bone dipped in sticky cactus sap. Full at last, Cror threw the bone into the lake. It landed on a bubble plant... and the bubbles washed away the sticky sap. Mazu had an idea! Just then, her friends and Totor arrived. "Hey guys, I think we can wash away the tar with that bubble plant!" she said. But before they could try, Giganto appeared. Cror tried to run, but ended up stuck to Giganto's tail. Now three dinos were stuck together!

Giganto shook his tail angrily.

"Wooaah!" screamed Mazu and Cror. If Mazu's plan was going to work, she and Cror had to work together.

"You've got to trust me," said Mazu. So when Rocky threw the bubble plant to Mazu, Cror flipped it with her tail for Mazu to catch. Next, Mazu held the plant near a hot spring. As if by magic, the bubbles melted away the tar – Mazu and Cror were unstuck at last!

"We did it!" said Cror proudly.

The next day, Mazu had a present for Cror. Mazu's special raptor reacher would help Cror to reach fruit high up in the trees. Now she wouldn't have to steal other dinosaurs' snacks any more!

"I'm glad we were stuck together, I got to know you a little better," smiled Mazu.

"You're not a bad dino, just a hungry one!" Cror smiled proudly. She couldn't wait to show Totor her very first present from her very first friend.

DINO DOOR HANGER

Make this great double-sided door hanger for your room!

1. Ask an adult to help you make your door hanger. Cut along the dotted lines.

2. Don't want to cut up your book? Just photocopy or scan and print pages 57 and 58 and stick them together instead.

3. Place the hook part of the hanger on your bedroom door handle!

Ask an adult for help making your door hanger!

SHHH...

DON'T WAKE GIGANTOSAURUS!

KEEP OUT...
GENIUS INVENTOR AT WORK!

TRUE OR FALSE?

See how many of these tricky Gigantosaurus questions you can answer correctly!

1. Gigantosaurus is always hungry? TRUE ☐ FALSE ☐

2. Is Gigantosaurus the most dangerous predator in the Cretaceous period? TRUE ☐ FALSE ☐

3. Gigantosaurus has four toes on each foot? TRUE ☐ FALSE ☐

4. Gigantosaurus is vegetarian? TRUE ☐ FALSE ☐

5. The colour of Gigantosaurus's skin is blue? TRUE ☐ FALSE ☐

6. Gigantosaurus lives in a lake? TRUE ☐ FALSE ☐

7. Gigantosaurus is scared of Bill? TRUE ☐ FALSE ☐

8. Gigantosaurus has spikes on his back? TRUE ☐ FALSE ☐

Answers on page 77.

ALL ABOUT... DINO FRIENDS

There's nothing we like more than having lots of fun with all of our dino friends. Let's find out about them!

TREY

Tiny's teenage big brother. Trey can't understand why his little sister wants to be an artist instead of a fearsome warrior.

ARCHIE

A nervous archaeopteryx. He tries his best to fly at the first sign of trouble, but his wings just don't seem to work like they should!

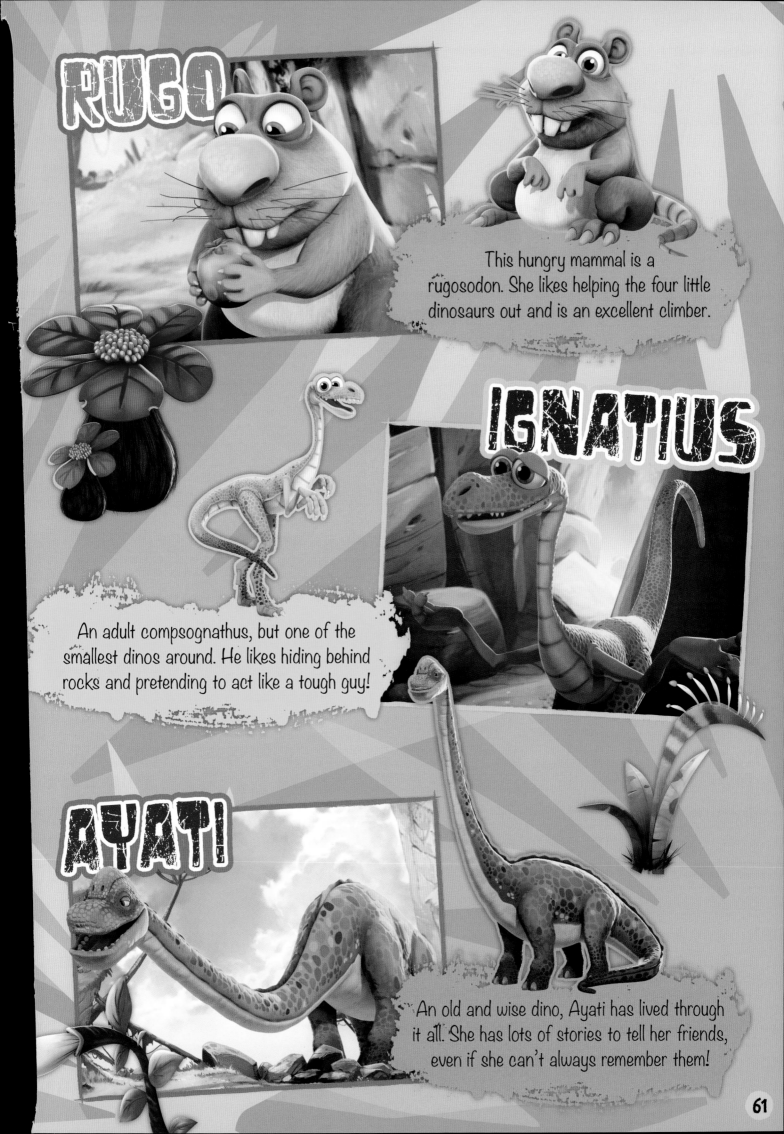

RUGO

This hungry mammal is a rugosodon. She likes helping the four little dinosaurs out and is an excellent climber.

IGNATIUS

An adult compsognathus, but one of the smallest dinos around. He likes hiding behind rocks and pretending to act like a tough guy!

AYATI

An old and wise dino, Ayati has lived through it all. She has lots of stories to tell her friends, even if she can't always remember them!

MARSHALL

Although larger than his four dino friends, 'Marsh' is just a big kid. He's also very strong and can throw things far with his spiky tail!

HEGAN

A grown up pterosaur with massive wings. She flies her friends all over the place and likes spending most of her time in the sky.

PATCHY

Make sure not to stray into Patchy's territory or he might just try to ram you with his boney egg-shaped head!

DILO

Dilo likes nothing more than playing sneaky tricks on other dinos. It's a good thing they usually backfire and he gets tricked!

ARTHROPLEURA

This scuttling centipede-like creature can be seen scuttling all over Cretacia. They're handy for fast travel too!

DIPLOCAULUS

A young dino, Diplocaulus loves playing games in the water. If you throw something, he'll catch it and bring it right back!

MAZU'S MEMORY TEST

Study the images on this page for two minutes. Now cover up the page and see if you can answer the tricky questions below!

1. Is Hegan standing on a rock?

2. How many dinosaurs are flying in the sky?

3. Is there a waterfall in the picture?

4. Does Rocky have his hands on his hips?

5. How many dinosaurs are in the boat?

6. Is Gigantosaurus in the picture?

Answers on page 77.

CRETACEOUS COLOURING!

MAZU

Use all of your favourite pens, pencils and paints to colour in this picture of best pals, Rocky, Bill, Mazu and Tiny!

TYRANO TREASURE HUNT

BILL

Can you find all of these items hidden in this scene? Use the checklist to tick them off!

Answers on page 77.

ALL ABOUT... MONSTER MEANIES

ROCKY

It's not always fun and games in Cretacia. These mean menaces are always out to get us when we least expect it!

TOTOR

This bumbling bully keeps coming up with cunning plans, even though they usually backfire. He and his sister often aren't half as clever as they think they are!

CROR

A sneaky velociraptor, Cror and her bother Totor think they're masters of the jungle, but this sneaky pair can usually be outwitted.

CARNIVOROUS PLANT

Its roots might mean it's stuck in one place, but this hungry plant still has plenty of bite. Watch out for the kissing version too!

GIANT SCORPION

Usually found in the deserts of Cretacia, these huge armoured creatures have a mean sting in their tails!

TERMINONATOR

A huge sea reptile also known as a plesiosauroidea. Watch out when you're near the water or she might think you're a tasty treat!

71

DREAM DRAWINGS

What do you think Giganto dreams about when he's sleeping? Fill these bubbles with your dino dream doodles!

ROARing loudly!

Eating a bone!

Stomping around!

TINY'S DINO JOKES

Tickle your friend's funny bones with Tiny's hilarious dino jokes!

What do you call a dinosaur with no eyes?
Do-you-think-he-saurus?

What did the dinosaur put on her steak?
Dinosauce!

What makes more noise than a dinosaur?
Two dinosaurs!

What do you call a sleeping dinosaur?
A dino-snore!

What was T-Rex's favourite number?
Eight (ate)!

Why should you never ask a dinosaur to read you a story?
Because their tales are so long!

What do you call a T-Rex who hates not winning?
A saur loser!

What do you call a dinosaur that never gives up?
Try-try-try-ceratops!

What does a triceratops sit on?
It's tricera-bottom!

What did the T-Rex say at lunch time?
Let's grab a bite!

ROCKY

ULTIMATE GIGANTO-QUIZ!

How much do you know about the world of Giganotosaurus? See how many of these fun questions you can answer!

1

What is the name of Mazu's vehicle?

a. Mazcar
b. Maztrike
c. Mazmobile

2

What kind of animal is Rugo?

a. Mammal
b. Lizard
c. Insect

3

Where do the dinos all live?

a. Jurassica
b. Cretacia
c. Triassica

4

What is the name of Totor's sister?

a. Archie
b. Cror
c. Hegan

5

How old is
Rocky?

a. 5 years old
b. 3 years old
c. 9 years old

6

What's Bill's
favourite thing to do?

a. Sleep
b. Draw
c. Eat

7

What does Tiny
really not like to do?

a. Paint and draw
b. Make cakes
c. Have a mud bath

8

What kind of
dinosaur is Mazu?

a. T-Rex
b. Brontosaurus
c. Ankylosaurus

10

Which of these
dinosaurs is the oldest?

a. Mazu
b. Marshall
c. Ayati

9

What does Giganto
do when he's asleep?

a. Growl
b. Snore
c. Hiccup

Answers
on page 77.

HOW DID
YOU DO?

1-2 correct: Good try!

3-5 correct: You know your dinos!

6-10 correct: You're ROAR-some!

75

ANSWERS

PAGE 15 - WORD SEARCH CHALLENGE

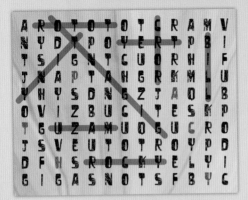

The secret character is Patchy.

PAGES 16-17 - DINO DIFFERENCES

PAGE 18 - WHO'S THAT DINO?

The dino is Marshall.

PAGE 19 - MARVELLOUS MAZE

PAGE 29 - ODD ONE OUT

Pictures 1 and 5 are the same.

PAGE 39 - SNEAKY SHADOWS

1 - D
2 - E
3 - A
4 - B

Shadow C is the odd one out.

PAGE 46 - SMALL AND TALL!

1 is the biggest and 3 is the smallest peach.

1 is the biggest and 4 is the smallest egg.

5 is the biggest and 3 is the smallest dragonfly.

PAGE 47 - CRETACEAN CLOSE UP

1. Bill   3. Trey   5. Rugo
2. Mazu   4. Cror   6. Patchy

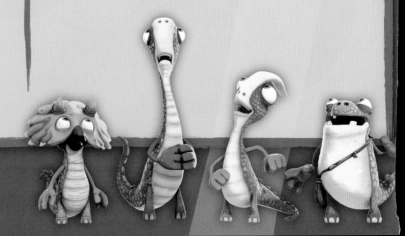

PAGE 48 - CRAFTY COUNTING

PAGE 49 - PREHISTORIC PATTERNS

PAGE 56 - DINO DETECTIVE

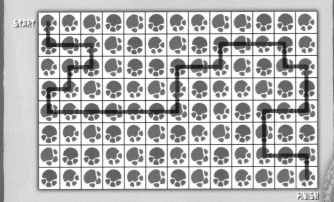

PAGE 59 - TRUE OR FALSE?

1. True	3. False	5. False	7. False
2. True	4. False	6. False	8. True

PAGE 64 - BIG PICTURE, LITTLE PICTURE

Picture 3 does not appear in the big picture.

PAGE 65 MAZU S MEMORY TEST

1. Yes, Hegan is standing on a rock.

2. There is one dinosaur flying in the sky.

3. Yes, there is a waterfall in the picture.

4 Yes, Rocky has his hands on his hips.

5. There are four dinosaurs in the boat.

6. No, Gigantosaurus is not in the picture.

PAGES 68-69 - TYRANO TREASURE HUNT

PAGES 74-75 - ULTIMATE GIGANTO QUIZ!

1 - c. Mazmobile	6 - c. Eat
2 - a. Mammal	7 - c. Have a mud bath
3 - b. Cretacia	8 - c. Ankylosaurus
4 - b. Cror	9 - b. Snore
5 - c. 9 years old	10 - Ayati